A modern approach

Reading and writing should flow through the natural activity and interests of the child. The next most important aid is a series of books designed to stimulate and interest him and to give daily practice at the right level.

Educational experts from five Caribbean countries co-operated with the author to design and produce this Ladybird Sunstart Reading Scheme. Their work has been influenced by (a) the widely accepted piece of research *Key Words to Literacy*[1], adapted here for tropical countries. This word list has been used to accelerate learning in the early stages. (b) The work of Dr Dennis Craig[2] of The School of Education, U.W.I., and other specialists who co   in areas where the Englis   ht to young childre   on entering school is a p   ing considerably from Standard Eng

1   *Key Words to Literacy*, by J McNally and W Murray, which was published by the Schoolmaster Publishing Co. Ltd., England.

2   *An Experiment in Teaching English*, by Dennis R Craig, which was published by the Caribbean Universities Press, also Torch (vol. 22, No.2), Journal of the Ministry of Education, Jamaica.

The Ladybird Sunstart Reading Scheme consists of six books and three workbooks. These are graded and written with a controlled vocabulary and plentiful repetition of the most used words in the English language. They are fully illustrated.

Book 1 *Lucky dip* (for beginners) is followed by book 2 *On the beach*. *Workbook A* is parallel to these and covers the vocabulary of both books. The workbook reinforces the words learned in the readers, teaches handwriting and introduces phonic training.

Book 3 *The kite* and book 4 *Animals, birds and fish* follow books 1 and 2, and are supported by *Workbook B*. This reinforces the vocabulary of books 3 and 4 and again contains handwriting exercises and phonic training.

Book 5 *I wish* and book 6 *Guess what?* with *Workbook C* complete the scheme.

The illustrated handbook for parents and teachers is entitled *A Guide to the Teaching of Reading* The flash cards produced for Sunstart's parent scheme, *The Ladybird Key Words Reading Scheme* support the reading process.

Published by Ladybird Books Ltd
A Penguin Company
Penguin Books Ltd, 80 Strand, London WC2R 0RL, UK
Penguin Books Australia Ltd, 707 Collins Street, Melbourne, Victoria 3008, Australia
Penguin Group (NZ) 67 Apollo Drive, Rosedale, North Shore 0632, New Zealand

018

© LADYBIRD BOOKS MCMLXXIV, this edition MMVI

ISBN-13: 978-1-84422-669-6

Printed in China

Ladybird
Sunstart

Lucky dip

BOOK 1

written by W. Murray
illustrated by Martin Aitchison

Talk about the picture

Tell the story

Talk about the pictures

Learning colours

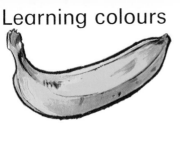

LOOK and find
another like this

and this

and this

and this

boy

girl   bird

boy   man   box

girl   a girl   boy   a boy

a girl

a boy

new words   a   girl   boy

a girl   a boy

a girl

and

a boy

I see a boy and
I see a girl.

I see

big girl   little girl   big boy   little boy

I see

a big girl.

I see

a little boy.

new words   big   little

big boy   big girl   little boy   little girl

You see the big boy and

you see the little girl.

---

new words   You   you   the

the boy   the girl

a bird

You see
the little boy
and
the big girl.
You see
a bird.

new word   bird

tree

a tree

the tree

Look at
the tree.
Look at
the big tree.
Look at
the little bird.

new words   Look   at   tree

2

two

Look at the boy
in the big tree.

You see two birds
in the big tree.

The boy sees the birds
and the two birds
see the boy.

---

new words   in   two

A boy is in
the big tree.

A girl is in
the little tree.

is

1
one

2
two

You see one bird.

You see one girl.

You see two boys.

The two boys look
at the bird.

one

Come and see.

You come and see it.

Come and see the Lucky dip.

Look at that.

Can you see that?

That is it.

That is the Lucky dip.

new words   that   That   Can

The girl comes.

She comes to look.

She can see it.

Can you see it?

Can you see
the Lucky dip?

---

new words   She   to

The boy comes.
He comes to look.
He can see it.
You can see it.

He

box

The boy and the girl want a box.

He says, I want a box.

She says, I want a box.

new words   **want**   **box**   **says**

a man

The girl says to the man
I want a box, please.

One for you,
the man says.

new words   man   please   for

Lucky

Thank you, says the girl
to the man. Thank you.

Look, she says
to the boy.

Look at that.

Thank

The boy says to the man.
I want a box, please.

One for you,
the man says.

Thank you, says the boy
to the man. Thank you.

Look, he says
to the girl.

Look at that.

Words used in this book

Cover: Lucky dip

Total number of words 34